THE BONDS IN CHRISTMAS

USA TODAY BESTSELLING AUTHOR

M.L. PHILPITT

AUTHOR'S NOTE

When I was writing The Sound in Silence, it dawned on me that after it, I would be working on The Obscurity in Wishing and that was the last planned/intentional time I would be seeing the Corsetti and Rossi families. That the series was nearly over but I truly felt like I wasn't done with them. They'd consumed my entire 2023 and letting them go felt impossible. But everyone's stories were done. The main plot was all wrapped up; all characters got their happily ever after.

I don't know at what point I opened up a new document and started writing Isabella and Rafael at Christmas time...and then it was another couple. Unintentionally, I'd written half a novella by this point. Then I finished it and it felt *right*. The Obscurity in Wishing *couldn't* be the series ending, but *this* would be. One last hurrah with all our couples, answering questions you might have had, such as:

- What happens to Della and Nico after the series, given they're running a mob family?
- What about the unanswered results of Ariella's infertility challenges?
- And more....

This novella answers all that.

The Bonds in Christmas is <u>NOT</u> a standalone. It is the series epilogue of the entire Fractured Ever Afters series therefore it's important/more impactful to read this after everyone's individual book. And there is a couple in here mentioned in The Hunt in Elusion and only shown in The Craving in Slumber so if you haven't read the start of the series, they will be unfamiliar to you. For complete background and understanding of this series, start with book 1, The Hunt in Elusion.

Triggers: recollection/mention of parental death, infertility, depictions of mental health & diagnoses.

Note, I'm Canadian. I write using Canadian/UK spelling. This means words will have U's in them, or double LL's. (colour, flavour, signalling, etc.) These are not typos.

For all the readers of the Fractured Ever Afters series.
This one's for you.
Happy Holidays!

RAFAEL

&

ISABELLE

Isabelle exits our bedroom and her heels make little noises as she walks down the hall. I stand from the couch to greet her, brought right back to months ago when I took her out on her first date, and what almost was our last.

The only mistake I've ever made, and the final one I'll ever make.

She breaks from the hallway and I lose my fucking breath at finally being able to see the dress she's hid from me for the past week, ever since her shopping trip in preparation for tonight.

A plain, black dress falling to mid-thigh covered in a gold chiffon, giving a shine to the entire thing. Its cap sleeves are high, the neckline low and granting me a view of her delicious breasts. My gaze finds the edge of her dress and follows her slim legs right down to the heels strapped to her feet.

"Ma belle." So many words, so many compliments flit through my mind, but they're all tied up as she approaches and rubs her palms up the front of my tux, making her own appreciative noises.

"I love seeing you in a suit."

"I wear one all the time." I reach out to stroke a rosy cheek, thrilled when her skin deepens. Even now, I can get her to blush so easily. One wouldn't think this is the same woman who can take my cock while being observed by strangers, based on how easily embarrassed she becomes.

She smiles and shrugs a single shoulder, drawing my attention to her smooth skin. I trail my hand from her face, down her neck, and gather the soft brown waves falling midway down her back.

"I know what I want for Christmas."

She giggles and shoulders away from my touch, shaking her head as she reaches for her small clutch she pre-prepared earlier. "You already have me."

I only have fifty percent of her, but after tonight, I will own the rest of her too. Her last name, finally transforming her from Isabelle Dupont to Belle Corsetti.

It's been almost six months since I bought her the ring, and it's been locked away in my desk drawer in Eden the entire time. Whenever I considered proposing, it didn't feel like the best time. Her grief over her father's death has been so fluid as well, so by the time I worked up the nerve to pop the question, her mood lowered, and I didn't want to add pressure or anything onto her.

Christmas seems a bit basic to propose on, but then I put together her gift, and decided, I don't care. When it comes to her, nothing else matters but her happiness.

I lead her to the elevator, tapping the button to take us only one floor down, immediately gaining her curiosity as the doors shut, move, and open just as quickly.

"Wh-what's happening? Aurora and Rosen are waiting downstairs. Aurora texted that she was on her way to the car a few minutes ago."

Since my sister and her ex-bodyguard moved in a few levels below us, it's become simpler to carpool when we head to the mansion. In the months since, it's also given Isabelle a friend, as she and Aurora have spent hours together. Belle's even joined her at the community garden a few times, and though Rosen typically drives them back and forth, occasionally I've gone myself, and damn, if seeing her crouched and playing with children doesn't make my heart burn with a new wave of longing.

I don't want children, not yet...but one day. Isabelle will be a damn good mother too. I can't imagine the number of children's books that'll eventually fill our house when she teaches them to read.

I tug her down the hallway to one of the condo doors. Of the few doors in this hallway, they all now lead to the same room.

"Hey, wait, wasn't this where a bunch of the construction noises were coming from?"

My answer is a grin over my shoulder. It drove her crazy, but I had them mainly work during the day when she was at her job in one of the city's library branches.

"You told me the last owners wrecked the place and you were having it renovated before selling it."

"Half-true," I admit. "I'm the new owner."

Her brows jump to her hairline. "You bought your own property?"

"Something like that." With the door unlocked, I step behind her and lift my hands to cover her eyes, lowering my head until I can whisper in her ear. "Door's open. Just push it."

Her hand stretches in front of her, blindly pushing it open, and once she does, I step into her back, forcing her into the newly-renovated condo, which has been completely gutted to be one giant room. The old kitchen platform has been redone with only a coffee and snack bar, and the bathroom remains, so she doesn't have to leave if she needs one. The windows taking up the far wall also remain and are now covered with sunproof, bulletproof, electronic shades. The rest of the walls are floor-to-ceiling bookshelves, with the centre of the room being a carpeted sitting area: a few different chair and couch styles, and tables, giving her the maximum opportunity for the prime reading positions.

It's better than the Corsetti's mansion library, if I say so myself.

"Merry Christmas, Belle."

And then I drop my hands from her face, her gasp almost instantaneously as she takes in the massive space, the numerous bookshelves that are only partially filled with books.

"What...you...oh my god."

"That is my name, yes," I say.

She takes three steps toward the bookshelves, and then pauses to glance at the sitting area and beyond, before back to the books. And finally, behind her, to me.

"How?"

"Oh, it's quite easy. Go." I jerk my chin toward the shelves. "Check them out. Reassure me I bought the correct books." I know I did. I hacked her reviewing account and bought a paperback of every single book she's rated four stars and above, that she hadn't already owned. "It was so tempting to have the books you already own brought down here, but it's not exactly easy to remove shelves and shelves of books from upstairs without you noticing."

She sputters a laugh before whirling around and throwing herself into my arms, planting a kiss on my lips. "Yeah, no, it wouldn't be." With that marvel in her tone again, she murmurs, "Rafael, you bought me a fucking *library* for my present. A *library*. I feel like my gift for you won't beat this at all."

Her gift will be seeing my ring on her finger, so she'll definitely beat this, but I remain silent on that fact.

"I want to stay here and read. And buy more books to stock the shelves, but if I do that, we'll never make it to Christmas dinner. And I really want to meet Hawke in person."

Yes. Hawke. They've spoken a few times over phone calls or video messages, when I introduced her to him, and even explained Hawke's lucky involvement in what I've been referring to as the worst day of my existence—when she was nearly permanently taken from me.

Nico invited Hawke to Christmas dinner, and much to every single person's surprise, he agreed. He and Willow should be arriving to the mansion soon, if they're not there already.

So while every naughty idea involving fucking her in her brand-new space and trying out all those sexy scenes she enjoys reading to me is very appealing, I also want to see Hawke. More so, I want him and Isabelle together; worlds colliding; my family complete.

But first, I release her, knowing the moment I do, her interest for her new personal library will win out, which it does. She turns back to the room, pacing a couple feet away, telling me now's the right moment.

Taking the ring box from my pocket, I drop onto one knee and click it open.

ISABELLE

A library. A fucking *library*.

Rafael gutted an entire condo he could have easily sold to another resident all to give me my own library, filled with books I love, with so much space for more. Given the size of these condos, it'll take me years to fill these shelves.

Challenge accepted.

The sitting area in the middle, and the coffee and snack area where the kitchen used to be, tell me I've taught Rafael enough about reading that he's foresaw all my possible needs.

I can't wait to read in here. I'd happily go get changed now to spend the rest of the day here. To open the shades and see the late December snow falling from the Montreal skyline, to make a cup of hot chocolate, and to curl up on one of the couches. A literal dream come true, if I also didn't actually want to attend his family's annual party.

"You realize, you've just lost your girlfriend to this room, right?" I tell him, amusement lightening my tone. We need to get going, but I can't tear my gaze away from the shelves.

"Losing my girlfriend was precisely the intention." He has a strange tone, which compels me away from the books, and I turn around.

If the library-condo-room wasn't surprising enough, finding him on one knee is. It's not his positioning having my attention though, it's the ring box in his hand.

"Rafael..."

"Belle." He stops, his tongue dabbing his bottom lip, his brow lowering a fraction. He's nervous; an emotion I've seen so few times on him. "Isabelle Dupont, I'm not asking you because as far as I'm concerned, we've been wed since the moment I let you walk away from me and realized precisely how it feels to lose half of my heart. I'm not asking you to marry me because I'm *begging* you to allow me to take you in the final way I've yet to. Since the moment you opened your front door and told me to get off your step, you intrigued me. I knew how right you were for me when my shy bookworm snuck her way deeper into a sex club and accepted me then. And you owned my heart since the second you were stolen from me. The moment I came into your life, I've only brought chaos, but *ma belle*, I'm pleading for you to allow me to continue that chaos right up until death takes us both. Here in my hand, I'm offering the symbol of forever. Marry me, Belle, and make me the happiest man on earth."

No *yes* is needed for all the reasons he's listed. In my heart, I've already said yes. Upstairs, months ago, on one of our couches, we accepted one another.

"I hated you for bringing all that chaos into my life," I reply with a slow, spreading smile to lessen the harshness of my words so he's aware I'm making light of things, "and I'd be honoured to continue that chaos with you up until death."

I hold out my left hand.

He removes the ring and places the slim band on my fourth finger. A large diamond surrounded by yellow gems. He's always enjoyed me in yellow.

Then he stands and yanks me to his chest in a heated, possessive and claiming kiss. He still grips my hand, tangling his fingers with mine as he walks us backwards until my back hits against the bookshelves.

"I know we have to go," he whispers in the space between our bodies, "but fuck them all if I'm to wait until tonight to fuck my fiancée."

Fiancée. I shiver. And he's my fiancé. Damn.

His hands cup my face, forcing me to look at him, as if there'd be anywhere else. "I fucking love you, Belle."

"I love you too."

His hand lowers to my dress and as much as I want to do this, I stop him with a slight shake of my head.

"I want to give you your present as well."

He brings my hand between us, the ring shining in the room's light. "Believe me, you already have by allowing me to place this on your finger. There's nothing else I want."

"Nothing you want, but you'll enjoy it nonetheless." It took a lot of planning to get his gift done without anyone spoiling it to him, or for him to spot it himself. "I need my hands back." I tug against his hold.

Pouting, he releases me and the weight of my finger really settles as I use my hands, bringing them to the back of my dress, to unzip it beneath his amused and watchful gaze.

"Hm. I take it back. I think I'll very much want this present."

I laugh, and with the zipper lowered another inch, I'm able to drop the dress entirely, a new wave of nerves coursing through me. What I did —what I had done yesterday—I didn't think I'd *ever* do. Dad would have had a heart attack if I even asked.

Gravity takes the dress to the ground and I turn slightly, so he can see the right side of my body.

The tattoo on my ribs.

His mouth slips open, his hand stretching for me, and tracing the skin an inch away, aware from his own tattoos, how painful they can be. According to Rozelyn, who took me to her and Flynn's artist, I chose one of the worst spots on my body for a first tattoo.

"Isabelle...fuck." His voice is thick. "My god, baby, I take it all back. This is a level of permanence my crazy ass mind craves."

The art, a few inches tall, a couple wide, of a red rose. Detailed petals because Rozelyn's artist is amazing. But instead of a straight stem, it curves, loops in the form of his name.

Rafael's it for me. If not his name, it'd be no one else's. There is no breakup for us. No divorce. He's mine and I'm his and the ring on my finger, the tattoo on my side, mark me as such.

His brows lower. "Wait, two days ago, I had you undressed at the club. When did you...yesterday?" When I nod, biting my lip, he pieces the rest together. "Last night you said you weren't in the mood. You wore one of my shirts to bed, and didn't want to shower with me." He flicks the tip of my nose with his finger. "Sneaky, Belle. Fucking love it. Who do I owe for taking you to get that?"

"Rozelyn. She brought me to her and Flynn's artist yesterday."

"She's getting a raise. A car. A mansion. It's hers, whatever she wants."

I laugh again, pressing my hand over his heart. "Always so dramatic."

"That's what you love about me." His expression falls serious and he cups my hips, bringing me right up against him. "Any minute, my sister's gonna start nagging us, but we're not leaving until I have something to hold me off until dinner."

He drops to one knee again and brings a hand up the inside of my leg until I shiver in desire, not fighting him as he lifts my leg, the shelves at my back keeping me steady.

"Hold on tight, *ma belle*. I need to show you how exactly a beast responds to seeing his marks on his beauty."

He covers my core with his mouth.

ROSEN

&

AURORA

"Fuck, could you two have taken *any* longer?"

I cover Aurora's knee with my hand, shooting her a warning look to not be rude to her brother. Rafael texted us hours ago to let us know his plans for Isabelle, and based on the rock on her finger, the red cheeks, and his messed-up hair, it worked out in his favour.

She pushes my hand away, glaring, and leans over the seat to put her face by Rafael's. "Seriously, Nico said to be there for two o'clock. It's already two now and we haven't even left yet."

Rafael leans over and drops a quick playful kiss on his sister's cheek, which only aggravates her further based on the grumble as she falls back in her seat beside me. "Since when are you so worried about timings?"

"Since we *all* agreed to be at the vehicle for one-thirty and it's, oh," dramatically she waves her phone in the air, "one forty-five. A-plus, you two."

Isabelle glances over her shoulder as Rafael starts the car and exits the underground parking lot of the condo building. "Sorry, Aurora, that might have been my fault. Once I showed him his birthday present, he—"

"Ugh, please, no!" Aurora jams two fingers into her ears. "I do not want to hear about *that*."

Isabelle laughs, shaking her head. "No, no. Well, yes...but no. What you're thinking was the outcome. I got a tattoo dedicated to him. I'll show you later."

That eases Aurora and she presses into my side, breathing deeply. "Okay then. I'll accept that. Not that we're late, but whatever."

Rafael meets my eyes in the rear view and I see his question as soon as he repeats it to her. "Again, what has you so worried about the time?"

She told me why earlier, but I won't share. Instead, I re-place my hand over her knee, sliding it up and down, easing her anxiety in a way I know she finds comfortable. After a few strokes, her shoulders lower with her deep breath and she tilts her face so I can read her lips.

Thanks.

I press a quick kiss there, responding with a silent, *My pleasure.*

"Dude," Rafael's loud voice chimes in, "seriously? She's my sister, and I'm right here."

"Coming from the guy who did nothing to hide the fact that he just had sex before joining us. Before you judge us, look in the mirror."

Rafael meets my eyes, narrowing them. "Yeah, well, when Aurora gets your name tattooed onto her skin, then you'll know how enjoyable the sight is. Shut it."

Aurora opens her mouth with a comeback, but I quiet her with a finger to her lips. Then I cup her head, keeping her on my shoulder as my hand continues its cycle, maintaining the calmness.

Today will be the first time she's seeing Hawke since Nico's wedding, and she woke up suddenly very anxious about it. Pleased, but worried. Maybe because Hawke agreed to come to Nico's Christmas celebration without any stipulations, fully aware their parents will also be in attendance. Aurora assumes today will end in an argument, and while holidays often bring family drama, for her, she doesn't want it. It's her first Christmas home since she was six, and she's spent all week telling me how she wants it to be calm, content, and pleasant.

"Also," I call up, "congrats you two."

"Thanks, man." Rafael grins, glancing at his new fiancée beside him before taking Isabelle's hand into his.

My hand slides from Aurora's knee to her clenched hands in her lap, rubbing over them in a calming manner. But really, I'm feeling her left hand, where I hope to place a ring eventually.

I already have it. Mom's ring, that Dad had given me. Said she'd love Aurora and would want me to pass it along. It's a smaller diamond than I would have preferred to buy because Aurora deserves everything I can provide. But the longer I stared at it, the more I imagined it on her finger, and the more perfect it became. Aurora isn't a showy person. She's happy in our condo, starting a diploma in childcare, and working away from everything her mafia family stands for. In some ways, she's similar to Hawke, which is likely where her deep-sated need for a relationship with him comes from.

Yesterday, we went to Dad's house for a Christmas Eve celebration, aware today would be spent with her family. One couldn't guess that a mafia princess was in attendance when she was seated on the floor playing toy cars with my nephew, Elliot.

It was the perfect holiday celebration and only made me fall in love with her deeper—something I hadn't known was possible. With Dad there, my sister, Poppy, her husband, and Elliot, it was everything to me.

Toward the end of the evening, Dad pulled me aside and gave me the ring box. Claimed he saw the way I was staring at Aurora all day and knew, soon, I'd be thinking about popping the question.

Thing is, when we got together after the De Falco drama that led to her coma and Nico learning about our relationship, I promised not to push her into anything, considering her family runs on one speed: quick. Our relationship could be paced and we'd get married eventually, when she's ready. She's still mine, and that's enough.

But seeing the engagement ring on Isabelle's hand has me thinking otherwise. I want my mother's ring on Aurora's hand. It may be old-fashioned but I want to switch her name from Corsetti to Carrigan.

So lost in thought, I don't realize we've arrived at the Corsetti mansion until Aurora pulls from my hold and is out of the car before Rafael fully parks. Despite the negative twenty-degree weather and foot of snow coating the driveway, she rushes to the front doors.

"Jesus," I curse, scrambling to follow while Rafael's loud laughter booms from the car. "Your sister's impossible to keep up with."

By the time she's pulling open the front doors, I catch up, and Isabelle and Rafael approach.

Isabelle glances between us and then her new fiancé. "You told me he used to be her bodyguard. How did you never lose her?"

Oh, I had. Lost her in a club once, which was the beginning of the end of my promises to her brothers.

The door opens to the Corsetti Boss and Aurora's brother, Nico, grinning. At his side is Della, who opens her mouth to greet us, but when a flash of black hair comes up behind them, Aurora shoves between them.

"Move it! I see you two all the time. Hawke!" Three steps in, she launches herself into her eldest brother's arms. "When did you get here? I wanted to be here for your arrival."

Hawke hugs her tightly, answering her, as Nico gestures for the rest of us to enter. I shed my coat, as does Isabelle and Rafael, and Della takes them to hang.

"Someone's excited." Nico nods toward his siblings. Hawke stands by Aurora since now his girlfriend, Willow, is also hugging her in greeting.

"Nervous actually," I murmur, not wanting Aurora's business to spread around. "She wants this to be a good Christmas, considering it's her first here since childhood."

Nico's mouth flattens, because he too disagreed with his parents' decisions. "We'll be sure to change that then. My parents have already arrived, as did the Rossis, and Rozelyn and Flynn. You're the only ones we were waiting on."

"Don't let Aurora hear you say that," Rafael comments, coming up behind us. "She bitched me out for taking too long giving Isabelle her gift."

"You mean the rock on her finger?" Nico slaps his brother on the back and leads the way down the hallway. "Took you long enough."

"Not everyone gets engaged after a week," he replies dryly, knocking on Della and Nico's quick engagement. Rafael had the ring made months ago, shortly after they officially became a couple, but he said he was waiting for what felt like the right moment.

I catch up to Aurora and Hawke, nodding a greeting to Willow. Aurora releases her brother and leans into my chest, whispering, "I already feel better."

"Good." With my finger, I tilt her head up, planting a kiss on her lips. "Now, be good for the rest of the day. Play nice with your family so I can reward you with my present tonight."

Her gaze grows heated and she leads me off to the side, so we're still walking down the hall but at a slower pace to avoid being overheard. "If it's a gift, I get it either way. My attitude changes nothing."

She'd be right if she hadn't made that very point. "Careful, *princesse*. The outcome is all dependant on you. Be a brat today, and I'll keep you on the edge until New Year's. Be good, and I'll have you coming so many times tonight, you'll think you have died and gone to heaven."

We enter the sitting room, where Mom and Dad immediately yank me into a hug, which I return. Seems like they hug me a lot now, like they're making up for the years they didn't. It's a bitter subject still, but I can't hate them for the past. Not when living in the present is so much nicer.

"You haven't had a Christmas here since you were a child," Mom states, her eyes misting. She blinks rapidly twice and smiles sadly. "Damn, I told myself I wouldn't do this today."

"It's okay," I tell them, looking between my parents. "It's okay because years without a proper celebration has led to this moment, and look." I break away from their hold to gesture to the sitting room.

To the crowd of people greeting one another. To Rozelyn and Yasmine both standing to greet Isabelle, and Rosen and Rafael joining the ex-De Falco sisters' husbands, Erico and Caladin, the New York *Famiglia* Boss and Consigliere, who seem less menacing with the Christmas lights acting as a cheerful backdrop. To the brother I lost, and the son they had, clutching onto his girlfriend's hand as he speaks to Nico and Della.

Family.

A weird combination of mobsters and outsiders alike, of enemies and allies, all under one roof.

"It wouldn't be *this*," I continue, bringing my attention back to my parents. "Honestly, I'm quite excited for all of us to be together after the year we've lived through."

"Survived through," my father interjects with a pat on my arm. Affection with him has been tougher over the past few months, but Nico mentioned that's simply Dad's way. Other than toward Mom, his penance for giving his children affection is less. He thinks it's due to the decades of having to wear a mask as Boss and not revealing his heart—his weaknesses.

Mom reaches for his hand and he brings it up to his mouth, kissing the back of it. They share a look I feel like an intruder on, so with a final parting smile, I tell them, "I'm happy to be here, Mom and Dad."

~

I spend most of the next hour with Hawke, since I see him less frequently. He and Rosen ended up in some long conversation about law that completely went over my head. Seated on one velvet couch, Hawke and Rosen beside each other, with me on Rosen's lap and Willow on Hawke's, I loved the connection.

Willow is a sweet girl. Someone I've met already but didn't have the chance for much conversation. It was somewhere between the terms *due process* and *appeal* that it struck me how much I truly enjoyed Hawke and Rosen getting along.

Because they'd be brothers-in-law eventually.

Willow would be my sister-in-law because, no doubt, they'll get hitched soon. In fact, I'm half surprised they're not already.

The room is all partnered up in the terms of marriage, all except us four and Rozelyn and Flynn. Isabelle and Rafael are now engaged, the Rossis both ended up with Ariella and Yasmine due to marriage deals, and Della and Nico's been married for a few months.

It was only a few short months ago that I told Rosen I didn't want to get married. I suppose, this environment changes shit.

In the past six months, I realized it's the ceremony I don't want. After being a part of Nico's grand wedding, it was too much. Worse, when back then, I should have had a repeat event with Erico one month later, so consider me traumatized against the whole concept. Besides, given the fact everyone I care about is in this room, who'd come? Nico would be obligated to invite all the important people in the organization, plus any allies and business partners, but they'd attend for him. It's a lot of fanfare for nothing. More so, it's not Rosen or me. We're not those people. We're simple.

That's what I want.

That's what I realized I want a few weeks ago.

"How's school?" Willow asks, pulling me from my musings.

"Good. Between semesters at the moment, but I'm enjoying it. It's only my first time doing such a thing, so I wasn't sure if I'd stick to it initially."

Yes, I thought that attending college for a diploma in childcare nearly sent my parents to their deaths. They ended up becoming pretty understanding to the ordeal, though, as long as I had a guard with me. Nico and of course Rosen were already all over that. With Rosen's new position as Capo, he couldn't very well follow me to class all the time—although, he certainly tried—so he stuck a literal army on me. Four different soldiers.

I smile and tell them it's fine, because it is. I'm doing what feels right. Between that and my constant trips to the community garden with Rozelyn, coming home to *our* condo with Rosen, making a life *I* want and no one pre-designed, is pretty fantastic.

Nico announces dinner's nearly ready then, and the energy shifts in the room. Couples re-partnering up to walk to the dining room. Willow stands and reaches for Hawke, who shoots Rosen and me a parting smirk as he follows her.

Beneath me, Rosen shifts, his arms tightening around my waist until I'm turning to see him. "How are you?"

He's actually asking: *how anxious are you?*

"I'm good." I lean into him, wrapping my arms around his neck as more people leave the room. Soon, we're the last in here, which works. "So caught up in all the joy."

Rosen reaches up to flick away strands of hair that fell into my face. "I'm pleased, Aurora. Truly happy."

He is happy—that much I can decipher. But there was another time I saw him this cheerful too. Yesterday, when we spent the day at his father's house. Me, him, his father, his sister, her husband, and their child. It was so nice to visit Elliot again, and we spent the entire day playing toy cars. I continued to watch Rosen from the corner of my eye, and no matter what I was doing—playing with his nephew or chatting with his sister—he was staring. At first, with love, and then at one point, I thought there was a flash of wistfulness.

Rosen moves to stand with me, but I urge him back to the couch. "They won't start without us. We're fine."

His eyes narrow playfully. "I'm hungry. Remember what I said about being good?"

"I'm trying to be, if you stay still. I'd like to give you your present."

And then I lift one leg and reposition myself until seated over him. His gaze drops to the space between my legs.

"With all three of your brothers next door and your parents, this isn't the most ideal place."

"It's the perfect place." I press my hips forward, grinding on him, aware by the instant flick of heat in his gaze what'll happen if I don't stop.

His hands clamp my hips and he leans into my chest, his warning growl imprinting against my lips. "I mean it. Stop, *princesse*, or do you need a reminder of my earlier threat?"

I'd rather come all night than be edged, so I push him away with a gentle swat and stop attempting to rile him up. "Okay, okay, you win.

Serious talk now." I reach into his pocket for my phone, which he's been carrying for me, and pull up his gift, booked a few weeks ago.

He takes the phone in first with a focused gaze, and then realization as he reads over the trip receipt for a week-long vacation in Fiji.

"We're going on a trip?"

"The fact your last vacation was...oh, never, you deserve it. It's cleared with my brother already." Which was more me telling Nico this was going to happen and less asking. "We're set to leave January second. Get out of this freezing city and into somewhere better. We'll be back the day before my next semester."

He smiles, his hands coming up my back to grip me tighter. "*Princesse,* I wish I got you something as good."

"Oh, but you will," I tell him with a sly grin. In truth, it's masking the fear. Not that I *don't* want to do this, but I honestly thought we'd be waiting a couple years. I'm making this decision because I want to. Because it changes nothing in my eyes, in my heart, but it'll be everything for my traditionalist man. "Because your gift to me will be to change my last name to yours."

His brows dip before smoothing almost as quickly. A glow from the overhead lights flicker in his gaze and his mouth parts. "Aurora..."

I shake my head, ending his doubts. "I want you, Rosen. You know it. I know it. This entire damn household knows it. What I don't want— what I avoided months ago—was a wedding. The fanfare. That's not us, and I'd prefer something that *is*. So, in Fiji, if we happened to elope on a beach beneath the sunset...I wouldn't mind."

Glee. That's what I see. What I expect to remain, but as quick as it does, it's gone and he looks away from me, to the empty sitting room. "Is this because of Rafael and Isabelle? Aurora, I'm happy to wait forever."

"No. Let's be honest. He had her ring months ago and waited. It could have happened on Halloween instead of Christmas for all we know, so it had nothing to do with them. No, I've been thinking lately, that's all. Thinking about the precise things I do and don't want, and the most certain *do* is you. As long as I can call you my husband without my brother or parents throwing some huge celebration to make it official in front of hundreds of people neither of us actually know."

This time, Rosen does let the doubts go. He hauls me to his chest, taking my lips in a heated kiss, only pulling back when I feel him hardening beneath me. Panting, he shakes his head and even slides me to my feet.

"Before that goes too far, we need to join dinner." He takes my hand, pulling me tight to his side. "I remember the first time we were in here. It was where we first kissed and I realized how utterly fucked I was. It's fitting in this room, we close another chapter of our lives."

"Close?"

"Yes, closing. We're opening the chapter where I get to call you my wife." And then he buries his head into my hair and growls in my ear. "Wife. *Ma princesse.*"

"Yours."

CALADIN
&
YASMINE

CALADIN

"Didn't know sneaking off was allowed."

I study the duo who've finally joined us. Aurora's cheeks flash red and she ducks her head as Rosen tucks her into the chair three down from the head of the table. He then takes the seat beside her and tosses a glare my way.

"Hey, now," I hold my palms up, "I just meant, had I known it was an option, I would have done it a while ago." I say that last part to Yasmine, who's also shooting daggers my way. Beside her, her sister is wearing a matching expression. "You all have no damn humour."

Nico's shaking his head at one end, waiting for me to shut it before he stands, garnering the attention of everyone at the long table.

He's at one end with Della to his right and Ariella on her other side. Erico's arm is positioned over Ariella's chair as he reclines back, watching the other mob boss in the room. I'm beside him, with Yasmine to my right, and I clutch her hand tighter into mine. She tosses a quick smile toward Rozelyn on her other side. Flynn's seated to Rozelyn's left, and to his right and at the opposite end of the table, the ex-Boss of this Corsetti clan, Lorenzo. To his right is his wife, Caterina, and beside her, the Corsetti Capo, Rosen. Aurora beside him, her eyes sweeping up and down the table like an overeager child. Beside her, the legend that is Hawke Corsetti, Blackwood as he now refers to himself, and his girlfriend, who's probably the frailest, quietest woman I've ever met—even quieter than Ariella, who's diagnosed with selective mutism—Willow. Isabelle, Rafael's now-fiancée is beside her, watching Nico with rapt attention. Rafael is the only one not watching his brother because with a lovestruck gaze, he's too preoccupied staring at his future wife.

Nico lifts a pre-poured wine glass in his hand. "I realize it's early in the evening, but I'd prefer to get the formalities out of the way now so we can all relax."

His gaze scans over everyone, landing on his brother last and clearing his throat. Without looking over, Rafael flips him the middle finger and even turns his body deeper into Isabelle, who nudges him away with a soft giggle.

Nico rolls his eyes but continues. "Less than a year ago, in a room only down the hall from us, a woman snuck into my house and changed my life in every way imaginable." He reaches for Della's hand, who gives it immediately, love shining in her gaze. "One might say she brought a battle onto this family, but all she did was help me realize the one we were already in. With her, our family expanded." His eyes shift to Ariella, and then down the rest of our side of the table, to Erico and me, and then to Yasmine and Rozelyn. "A sister who forged our group into another existing family. Stepsisters who joined us on both sides." His eyes flick over all of us again, and Yasmine's hand tightens in mine. I shoot her a look, catching her faint smile before she returns her attention to Nico.

I do too, but after another long stare. There's times I don't want to look away from her because while Nico's talking about the family Della has connected him to, Yasmine's done the same for me. Yeah, I've always had Erico, and up until a few months ago, his parents too, but it's not the same. It's not this.

"Della helped me see an issue that was already existing in my life," Nico continues. "An issue that led my brother, who refuses to pay me any attention, to his lovely fiancée." For that, he gains Rafael's notice, but through an eye roll and a cocky smirk as he leans away from Isabelle. "Della urged me to reach out to our older brother, and what's happening now is something I dreamed about for years."

I glance toward Hawke, who's staring at the serving plate in front of him. His ears, peeking from beneath shaggy, black hair, turn pink with the attention half the table sends his way. Willow reaches over to rub her hand down his leg, which seemingly breaks his concentration, but he doesn't look to her. He glances up at Nico, and then quickly down the length of the table to their parents, brows dipping with obvious troubled thoughts.

"Aurora returned to us, and made me realize that sometimes, I can't force a relationship. Sometimes it hits. Sudden, hard, with no way to stop it." Nico glances at Della again, his words obviously meant for her too, and once again, I relate. I get it. Yasmine was the force I never wanted, but now, wouldn't know how to survive without. "And then my parents. The matriarch and patriarch of this family for so long. Christmas wasn't always like this," he announces in a tone softer than before. "With everyone here, like this, but I want it to be. Every year, for the rest of our lives. Our large group, joined by blood, unions, love, two families, coming together."

He says the last part to Hawke, who subtly bobs his head. No one's paying attention to the eldest Corsetti sibling, but I am. I am, because his name was known for decades even within the *Famiglia* and the horrors of what happened to him, so it's admirable he's here. I haven't gotten the chance to have a long conversation with Hawke, but I'm interested in learning more about him.

I squeeze Yasmine's hand but glance at my cousin. Last Christmas, I got drunk in my condo and he was reading over contracts for pending deals. We didn't even visit one another. Not due to animosity or anything, but because we haven't celebrated the holidays in quite a while. Once, for the few years after moving in, his parents tried to force something, but they struggled more than anyone. According to

Erico, they were the very few times they spent any meaningful time together.

Before I was ten though, my parents always threw the best celebrations. They'd have over all the family—Erico and his parents included—and our mansion was so vividly decorated, it'd put a holiday store to shame. My mother adored Christmas and she and Father would often perform carols late into the evening after everyone had gone to bed. I enjoyed sneaking down and witnessing their displays of love and comfort with one another. I'd head to bed then, content with my life.

I glance at the woman beside me, who's become my new life. I want that with her. I want *this*, what Nico's offering. Everyone under one roof. For her to see her sister. And maybe one day, for her sister and Flynn to fly to New York and visit us. I want children that I can spoil, who'll grow up and sneak downstairs all to witness the shared love their parents have for one another.

That's what I want.

Family.

Throughout dinner, Caladin continued to throw me strange looks that we certainly will be talking about later because at this point, he's weirding me out.

As we eat, his hand keeps a grip of one of mine, his thumb stroking over my wedding band, proving to me he's still paying attention, even when he struck up conversation with Erico, or Hawke and Willow from across the table.

Meanwhile, Rozelyn's been unnaturally quiet, but I understand. The last Christmas celebration we had with one another was also spent with Dad. If that even counted as anything. Dad didn't decorate, and he made Della help the chef cook a meal. I remember Rozelyn taunting her as she made the table up before being forced to eat alone in the kitchen. Rozelyn had a guilty look buried in her eyes, just a flash, that I was feeling deep in my heart, even as I turned my head and ignored the room around me, all while Dad watched on without a care.

I glance down the table and spot Della speaking to Rafael. Like she knows my thoughts, her gaze suddenly darts over all the people between us and lands on me. She manages a small smile before returning to her conversation.

The plates are eventually cleared and the numerous desserts are laid out. Cakes and pies, cookies and other small treats, candies and chocolates, and in the centre of the table: a large tray of cinnamon-sugar covered deep-fried pastries, which I get the unpleasant honour of witnessing my husband practically climb the table to snag two.

"Yes!" he hisses like a child, enticing half the table to laugh at him as they retrieve their own preferred dessert.

I take a few cookies as well as a slice of apple pie, rolling my eyes as he devours the BeaverTails. In between bites, he mumbles, "I've missed these. They're so fuckin' tasty. I mean, you're all barbaric, but it's forgivable for the flavour."

"Barbaric?" Rafael echoes from down the table.

"Don't get him started," I plead. "Please. We'll be here all night on his anti-Canada tirade."

"I'm just sayin'," Caladin starts after his next bite. "You named a dessert after your *national animal*. That's weird."

Rafael shrugs. "It's the shape, man. Don't ask me. We didn't name it."

"No, but you eat it."

The two guys bicker back and forth on the dessert and eventually Rosen joins in too. "You're not wrong, Caladin. If we all think about it, it's a bit off-putting."

Caladin takes another exaggerated bite. "Off-putting but so fucking delicious too. You're forgiven. Up here, in the freezing temperatures, you're all bound to go a bit insane."

I nudge his shoulder, reminding him with my silent action that his own wife is Canadian, so to watch his words. "We're, like, an hour's flight above New York. The temperatures are basically the same."

"Nuh uh," Caladin rocks back into me, "it's Canada; therefore, it's colder by default."

"Your husband is so weird," Rozelyn announces loudly, stating the very thing I was going to. "But he's a good guy, so I can't fault him."

I'm *about* to agree but Caladin leans forward, catching my sister's attention. "It's 'cause I'm American."

She laughs, as does Flynn and the elder Corsettis, and soon even Hawke joins in, pointing at my husband with one end of his fork. "Except you're two Americans surrounded by fourteen Canadians. We'll bury you in so much snow, our polar bears won't even be able to dig you up."

Caladin's cheeks whiten and he returns to his "barbaric" dessert after a final look toward Hawke, enticing more laughter from the table.

"Ever thought it'd be like this?" Rozelyn asks, leaning forward to whisper in my ear.

"You asking if I ever believed we'd be a part of some huge ass dysfunctional family?" I voice her question in longer, descriptive terms. "Not even close, Roz. But you know, I think Mom would approve how our lives turned out."

Rozelyn glances to her right, to Flynn, and then around the table, landing last on Nico and Della at the other end. "I think you're right," she finally agrees.

The meal concludes and eventually people begin leaving the table, couples disappearing in different directions for post-dinner conversation. Before I manage to stand, Caladin snags my wrist and tugs me onto his lap, not caring about the audience still present. My arms rest around his shoulder to steady me while his arms bind my waist and his head drops into my neck.

"I love you," he states simply, whispered into my ear in a tone I'll relive for the rest of the night. "So fuckin' much, Yasmine. I didn't realize what I was truly missing from my life until you came into it, but it's this. Right here. A large family to celebrate with and a woman who's given me the world that I get to take home later."

My lips brush his forehead as his words lodge right into my heart. I feel the same. Christmas hasn't been good since Mom was alive, and even then...it wasn't this. It was strained by Dad's behaviour and attitude.

"I love you too, Caladin. You'll have this, always."

He lifts his head, shooting a blistering, possessive look my way. "As long as I always have you."

"Duh."

FLYNN
&
ROZELYN

FLYNN

The second Rafael and Isabelle stand from the table, it seems to signal the end of dinner, which I'm so fuckin' grateful for. I snatch Rozelyn's hand, *needing* her to follow, even if she'd much prefer to be around Yasmine for the time being. But I'm selfish, and for a few moments, I crave her company more than her sister ever will.

Enzo and Caterina both shoot me a knowing look, which I ignore and tug Rozelyn away from the table with a quick, surprised gasp. She follows me, recognizing my drive for escape. Because after these months together, she understands my demand for silence.

The second we're in an empty hallway, a few doors away from the dining room, I push her into the wall and cover her with my body, my head dropping into her neck. She strokes the back of my hair in a soothing, calm manner while I breathe her in.

"Too many people?"

In her neck, I rotate my head in a *no* motion while wondering the truth behind my answer. No, in the sense that the people at the table are all familiar to me, so they're not so bad to be around. Besides, their presence doesn't force me to speak with any of them, which meant through dinner, most conversation was had with either Rozelyn or Enzo and Caterina.

"Surreal," I mumble, pulling my head away to instead cup her cheek. "Sometimes, I wonder how my empty life would have gone on without you entering it."

The smile she did have falls, and I instantly hate myself for it. "What was Christmas like for you all these years?"

I look away, latch onto a spot on the floor by our feet, and it's that I answer instead of her. "I often went out. Driving everywhere and nowhere to escape. Caterina always invited me to her family's celebration, and all the Corsettis insisted I come. A few years ago, Nico even stationed men by the front entrance to ensure I wouldn't leave, so I snuck out another way."

Her frown remains, this time also tainted with sympathy, which I don't want or need. I chose to spend the holidays like that. It's not her doing.

"Why'd you avoid having family time?"

"Because as much as Enzo and Caterina tried, they weren't my family. Not really. While they cared for me, brought me in, I was never one of their kids. Wasn't like Nico or Raf, so I avoided it all. Let myself be alone because it was easier that way." With a hand on her neck, I angle her jaw, forcing her head up as my own attention finally unlocks from the ground. "I never *wanted* to have that happy family celebration until this year. Today. With you." But it felt good. Right. And I know by the pleasure that shone within Caterina's eyes when I told her we'd be joining them, she was more thrilled than anyone.

Rozelyn drags a hand up my arm, her palm to my cheek, so I turn my face into her hand to press a kiss there. "I'm glad, Flynn. You've never ever deserved to be alone."

I shrug. "If anything, it became familiar. Life growing up never gave me much in terms of childhood memories."

She frowns again. "I remember," she whispers, looking at the wall past me. "Do you? Remember, I mean. Remember Christmastime in high school?"

"It'd be impossible to forget," I tell her

When the halls were being decorated with stupid holiday décor the school's social committee dragged from back rooms and dusted off, they tried to make the place seem cheerful. More hopeful for those who had little—myself included.

It was the day before our two-week Christmas break and if I wasn't watching Rozelyn, I was staring at the clock, willing the arms to stop ticking by, knowing when one reached the twelve and the other the three, school would be over for two weeks, which meant two weeks without Rozelyn.

"Hardest time in my life," I muse, hauling her against my chest until our lips brush one another. There's a mark on her neck, left there by a chain from our play the other night. It's red, almost purple, and makes my cock hard remembering the gift she gave me then. "Also my best time too. It was impossible to let you go, considering you never let me near your house, but fuck, if I didn't cherish what you gave me that day, even when the guilt ate me alive."

Looking back, I now recall how much I despised that day actually. When she came to me with her present, I almost threw up. She was my girl and I couldn't get her *anything*. I wasn't creative enough to make her something. Had no job and no money to buy her a materialistic gift. And asking my father was way out of the question—not that he had any extra cash lying around either, considering he drank it all.

She shakes her head. "I wanted nothing then."

Then. That's the fucking part that eats at me now too. I drop my arms and back away, turning to stare in the opposite direction so she doesn't see the utter failure I'm being.

But my tenacious *soleil* follows me, her hand cupping my face to turn me around. "Whoa, Flynn, what happened? Something switched in you."

I jerk away from her touch, pacing a few feet, and stuffing balled fists into my front jean pockets. "Even then, you got me something. Something I—" The words, the truth, choke in my throat, but I swallow through the lump and admit, "I fuckin' cherished the lighter." She had it engraved with my initials because I always complained about having to steal a lighter from my father and it never being full enough of fluid. Even the hobby she despised, she respected enough to get me something I needed. "After I dropped out of school and quit smoking, I threw it away. It was the last thing of you I clung to, other than my memories, and it was an ongoing reminder of everything. You bought me a gift and I hated I couldn't afford to get you something then. For weeks, I've been wracking my head, Roze-lyn, to buy you the best thing ever, to make up for the numerous Christ-mases we've gone without, but *mon soleil,* I don't know what to get you."

She steps away from the wall, and I feel the heat of her skin. The scent of morning glory from her favourite shampoo. Another woman would reassure me. Mine just steps into my arms and rests her head over my heart.

"Flynn, I didn't buy you anything either. Despite dragging Della and Aurora to shop after shop, nothing felt right."

Maybe it's a bit fucked-up, but I laugh. Loud and booming and tighten my hold on the woman who's perfect for me. "So all my stressing is for nothing?"

She tips her head up. "Mine too, if it makes you feel better. *God*, do you know how fucking hard you are to buy for? More knives—boring. Clothing—not you. Jewellery—also not your style. Fuck off."

I laugh again, wrapping my hand possessively around the side of her neck, wary of the marks left there, as I back her into the opposite wall and cover her with my body. My hands wind around her wrists and I lift them until her back's arched into me.

"How about, we give one another a mutual present, downstairs in the basement. Since we moved out of here, I've been missing you down there."

Her mouth opens to respond, but the boisterous comment of my capo popping his head in robs me of her response. Rafael's grin says he's accomplished his goal of ruining this moment. "Hey, you two. People are wondering where you went." He studies the space between us—or the lack thereof—and waggles his brows. "Or want me to tell everyone you're busy?"

"Coming, coming." Rozelyn pulls out of my arms with a final heated smile, promising more after everyone's gone to bed. She strides by Raf and out the door, heading the way he came from.

Rafael lingers for a second, watching me. "You okay, man?"

"Yeah," I answer, and for once, my throat isn't filled with the lie. It's the truth when I repeat, "Yeah, I'm good."

The moment I make it back to the sitting room, I'm met with much more noise than earlier when everyone was in here. Clearly, after food and drink, celebration flows more freely. The first person I notice upon entering is Nico, who's holding an empty glass, his arm hanging over Della's shoulder, but based on the glazed smile she's sending his way, she doesn't mind. They glow in front of one of many Christmas trees the mansion is sporting. This one, a red and gold theme.

Across the room, Yasmine's chatting with Aurora and Rosen, but when she spots me, she murmurs something to them and rushes over.

"Where the hell did you disappear to?"

"With Flynn. Crowds sometimes make him anxious so a bit of quiet time before coming back into," I gesture toward the family around us, "this."

She's looking over my shoulder with a curious expression on her face, so I turn to see what's gained her attention. Flynn walks in, followed by Rafael, who steers him right toward Della, Nico, and Isabelle. Nico quickly hands him a drink of something dark and Flynn accepts it, but before sipping, finds me across the room.

Yasmine whistles, breaking my stare with him. "Light the room on fire, why don't you? Still surreal you two found each other after all this time."

"You and me both. That's actually what we ended up talking about. The one year I spent in the public school, during Christmastime, I got him something and he hated not being able to return the favour."

"Wait..." Her eyes dart to the corner, narrowing. "Was that the time you and I went shopping at the mall to get gifts for our parents?"

"It might be."

She snaps her fingers, the day returning to her. "When you totally abandoned me in a store because you were, in your words: 'heading to the bathroom. Will be five minutes.' And then you were gone almost a half-hour! Bitch."

I laugh, nudging her with my arm. "I didn't know what to get him! I had to look, and I couldn't trust you not to say anything."

She sticks her tongue out. "In another lifetime, that would wound me."

"Not now?"

She shrugs one shoulder. "Everything was different back then. Us, our situation, everything. It worked out for the best." She pauses, glancing down at my hands and then across the room. "Did you get him a duplicate gift this year?"

"Got him nothing," I admit, saying it aloud a bit easier than it would have been earlier in the week. "The gift then was a lighter engraved with his initials but now he doesn't smoke any longer. I couldn't figure it out and turns out, neither could he. But you know, gifts don't mean shit. Not really. Having him is all I wanted."

Yasmine grins in the way only an annoying little sister can, and it reminds me of growing up with her. "Thought I was the sappy one?"

"What makes you think that? Just because you're getting married for a second time and I'm not even doing it once?"

Yasmine glances at the new ring on her hand, given only a couple weeks ago when she and Caladin went on a Caribbean trip. It's a gold band with a turquoise gemstone, much more fitting for her than the plain diamond ring Caladin initially bought her after the marriage contract between him and the Seven.

She glances from it to Flynn, and then to me. "You think in the future, you two...?"

The future is unknown. Ask me a year ago if I believed we'd be standing in the middle of the Corsetti mansion as welcomed guests and not enemies walking a death march, and the answer would have been a big, fat no. But life's finicky, and here we are. But this, I know the answer to.

"No. That's not Flynn. I don't care otherwise. The bond between him and me goes deeper than a ring and a few vows." I glance at the new ring again on my sister's left hand. "No offence."

She chuckles. "None taken. I get it. I'd say the same if it wasn't for marriage making me fall in love. You're lucky and got to go about it the other way. If it's not for you two, like you said, you've vowed yourselves to one another in other ways."

"Yeah," I murmur my agreement, finding Flynn breaking away with Nico and Rafael who head to Hawke and Willow. He looks my way, somehow knowing I was watching him, and the look he shoots my way leaves no doubt of the permanence between us. "Besides," I continue, "is marriage all it's cracked up to be? I mean, look at our parents. We didn't exactly grow up with the greatest examples of marriage. Dad wed twice to further his own ploys." He might have actually grown to love our mother, but it's not a true love. Not like that around me.

Not even like Lorenzo and Caterina Corsetti, who Yasmine and I grew up hearing being referred to as the enemies. Whatever happened throughout their mob-style marriage, they've stuck it out. Had numerous children and, unless they're faking the love within both their gazes, found peace in this chaotic life.

Mom and Dad might have fell in love, but it's not like *that*. Pretty sure, Dad isn't even capable of such deep emotion.

The mention of Dad makes the chain in my pocket feel heavier. The very chain Nico once handed me, in which a tiny vile filled with Dad's ashes dangles from. After I shot him dead and the Corsettis were disposing of his body, it was Flynn's idea to cremate Dad and make three of these necklaces—one for Mom's grave, one for Yasmine, and one for myself.

From the moment Nico gave them to me, I was lost in what to do with mine. After everything Dad did to me, to my family, a huge part of me wanted to toss it in the Lachine Canal, to never be seen again. But it's at Flynn's insistence mine is presently locked inside a jewellery box, wrapped in some of Flynn's old sweatshirts, and buried within our lowest dresser drawer where I can pretend it doesn't exist.

To throw it away feels wrong, so I do agree with Flynn on that point, but to keep it out in the open is a betrayal to our happiness.

I ended up taking Nico up on his offer to have one buried with Mom because I believe she would have wanted it, but Yasmine's I hung onto. Even after Caladin retrieved her from British Columbia, my nerves never allowed me the courage to hand it over.

Tonight, I mean to. But I've yet to reach my hand in my pocket and retrieve it. To have Dad *here*, amongst everyone, seems like a betrayal. And honestly, I'd like to pretend to *not* be carrying it, even if it's for Yasmine to decide what to do with.

But as I study her contented expression again, pure glee glistening in her eyes as she takes in the holiday celebration around us, the Christmas décor throughout the sitting room, I *can't* remind her of the dark times in our history. Not now. Not today. For my sister's happiness, she deserves today. Choosing to keep a physical memento of Dad can be tomorrow's decision.

Two figures come up beside us then: Ariella and Della, and I've never been gladder for a distraction than I am now. Ariella smiles but Della murmurs her greeting, giving me something to focus on that isn't the necklace in my pocket or my guilt.

"You two okay? I'm happy you and Caladin were able to come up, Yasmine." She glances my way. "And that Flynn and you joined. I know, stuff like this is sometimes hard for Flynn but the others are excited to have him here. And I'm, well—"

In the months passing, Della and I have healed a lot of the animosity between us. I've grown closer to Aurora than her, mainly due to our shared interests with the community garden and the kids, and that's how it'll likely always be, but regardless, I've managed to gain a lot of time with Della. We're...okay. Nothing was forgiven instantly, but Della's heart of gold won out. She understood and forgave me for everything, much quicker than I would have, had I been in her position.

"Yeah," I finally agree, smiling back. "Me too, Della. Me too. You've said in the past, we're more family now than we were when our parents got together. I'd never agree with anything more."

I find Flynn's gaze across the room. If I had to do it all again, I'd let history repeat itself, all for this outcome.

ERICO
&
ARIELLA

ERICO

I'm standing by the fireplace with Caladin and Rosen, listening in as they debate which is a better weapon: a Glock or a Beretta. But only half my attention is on them, the remainder scanning the room over and over.

My parents would roll over if they realized where Caladin and I were. In their opinions, right in the centre of the monster's den: the Corsetti property. If a battle broke out, Caladin and I would be captured and killed in an instant; two against an army being an impossible fight.

But *if* isn't even an option, which is why I'm not concerned and why I mentally chuckle at how Father would react if he learned. He hasn't checked in since I banished him and Mother, and I haven't reached out.

Once, I'd be insane for being so comfortable on another mob's territory, but it's not like that anymore. It's weird to think, but Nico and Rafael Corsetti are more than forced allies through a union. I trust them. Trust them enough that I can lower my guard around them.

Which is why Caladin's a few drinks in and I'm not concerned about him. Why I'm even nursing my second whisky. Why we took Nico up on his offer to spend the night here. If it means Ariella has more time with her family, then happily.

She meets my smile from across the room where she's speaking to Della, Yasmine, and Rozelyn. She knocks me off my feet with every look, but this time, it's Della who gains my attention. When she glances between me and her sister and back before murmuring to the trio.

She breaks off and strides toward me, her gait and expression both focused, and I'm struck with how similar she and her sister actually are when they want something.

"Can I talk to you?" she asks in a demanding tone that even halts the conversation between Caladin and Rosen.

"Sure." I gesture for her to lead the way to the other side of the room but instead, she wraps her arm around mine and drags me from the sitting room and into the hallway. I meet Ariella's confused gaze on the way and only shrug. "Um," I start once we're in the hall.

Della turns one direction and drops my arm. "I wanted away from everyone in case we're overheard."

I fall into step beside her, our gait slow and mindless down the stretch of house. Her hands knot in front of her chest, not hiding her anxiety. "Makes sense. What's on your mind?"

"Ariella. How is she? I mean, like...with everything." She stops walking, tipping her head to show me her eyes nearly shiny with building tears. "She said she's fine, but she's hidden so much from me in the past, I genuinely don't believe her. Not about this. God, Erico, it's so fucked what's happening to her. She's been updating me with every appointment she has for another test but...I don't believe it."

Oh. I look away, toward the doorway we came from. Where my wife is living the worst pain imaginable. Years of dreaming of her own family, of being married and creating a happy family, all for a single customary test the *Famiglia* doctor ran to reveal she's infertile.

It crushed her. I'd say, it broke her, but broken implies she's no good anymore. That's not the case for her at all. It shattered her dreams momentarily, but with every passing test, she's becoming stronger and stronger. It's not breaking her; it's building her. Giving her a chance to tape herself up.

Not to say her depression diagnosis doesn't try to battle her every step of the way. Her dark shadows, as she describes them, consume her all over again after every unsavoury result. And there's been many of them. Multiple tests ran, multiple negative outcomes.

The last doctor recommended we give up. *"What you're doing is admirable and I understand wanting multiple opinions. Hell, I'd recommend a second, third, and even fourth before calling it...but a dozen? Now you have to consider your wife's mental health."*

I didn't tell her that. Couldn't. It was a month ago since the last test and in some ways, I took his advice. So far, I feel like I've hired every fertility specialist in the world. Every fucking doctor my money can buy. They've all given the same outcome.

I told her I refuse to give up...but is accepting giving up?

"Erico?"

"I think fine is the correct description," I finally answer. "She is, truly. She doesn't even cry anymore because she expects the outcome. Nothing's a surprise. But she's also not well." Admitting this feels like a betrayal of her secrets, but I know Della won't say anything. She's being her sisterly self and if I had a brother, I'd want him to do the same. "She's going to make it through this."

"I know. It's difficult to hear about the appointments and then be brushed aside when I ask her how she feels." She pauses, teeth scraping her bottom lip. "Does she at least talk to you? Basically, I'm making sure she isn't bottling them up, that's all."

Ariella and I have an agreement where she'll tell me when her feelings get low and we do talk after every test. She might not cry through them, but she's affected. Her sobs silent. Her tone dead. She informs me so I can be there and support her.

"She talks to me," I reassure Della. "It is hard on her, and I think she's giving up."

"Is there *any* chance at all? You haven't even gotten a maybe?"

I shake my head, unable to speak the words.

She looks away and curses. "Sorry to you, too. This affects the *Famiglia*."

"Only because so much of my focus is on her and not work, but the benefit of my role, is I don't care that it is."

The emotion clears from her eyes and she rips her head up, studying me with the same intensity Ariella does. "You really mean that, don't you? That heirdom isn't your focus?"

"With everything I have. There's one more option I'll be offering her so this isn't over...but yes. Her well-being and happiness matter more than the organization. Now that Caladin has Yasmine, perhaps they can provide the Rossi heir, worst case. If not," I shrug, "guess it gets handed off."

She blinks. Once, twice. "Um. Wow. You're so open." Her laughter is huffed and yeah, I might have spoken too openly about *Famiglia*. Blame the alcohol. Blame the fact that she's looking at me with the same damn expression her sister gives me. "Well, thanks for letting me pick your brain. I'm glad she has you." She turns for the direction we came from. "That's all. We can go back now."

I reach for her elbow before she gets too far. "Could you send her out here? I'd like to speak with her."

Della smiles. "Of course."

ARIELLA

After Della directed me toward the hallway with a watery smile, I know *something's* up. After all, she disappeared with Erico. Only for about five minutes but it's odd. Unless Della was yelling at him about stealing me away, the two haven't ever had long conversations.

I find him leaning against the wall about ten feet from the room we've all been hanging out in. He grasps my face as soon as I'm in an arm's reach and tugs me into his kiss. But when he pulls back, it's not love I see.

It's an apology that causes my stomach to drop.

"What is it?" I whisper, not wanting the answer myself.

He glances up and down the hall, even though we're alone. "There somewhere we can talk in private?"

We're near the library, so I bring him in there, recalling the only handful of instances I've ever come in here. There's a sitting area in the centre with three couches and tables that I lead him to. Only he stands while I sit and begins pacing up and down the carpet.

"Erico?"

"I wanted to do this today because if you need support from

someone that isn't me—if you need your sister, or Caterina, or anyone not me, then they're here for you."

The weight gets worse, dragging my stomach to my feet. There's only one topic he'd suggest using other's support to get through.

My hand rests over my stomach. My flat stomach. Forever flat according to the numerous doctors...

"But we don't have to, if you don't want to."

"Just say it," I manage no louder than a whisper. My throat won't allow for louder. Hiding from the truth even now.

"I don't want to lower your mood on such a happy day."

"Erico," I snap in a bit firmer tone. "Tell me what you learned." It's been a month since the last test. Erico claimed he's still hunting for another specialist, so maybe this is the unfortunate news that he couldn't find someone.

Erico stops pacing. Stares at me. Steps closer. Then drops to his knees and rests his head on my lap, his arms around my waist and hugs me to him like I'm a lifeline he's clinging to.

He's affected too and I'm a bitch for never checking on him. Every appointment, he's right there, helping me through it, but this is having a toll on him too, and I'm witnessing that toll.

Fingers through his hair, I brush strands off the back of his neck and curl over him, hugging him back. Sitting in silence for however long he needs.

It's ten minutes later when he lifts his head and his eyes are watery, red-rimmed, and they lock on my stomach. Slowly, after another agonizingly long five seconds, he rests a large hand over it.

"You have no fucking idea, Ariella, how much this kills me to not give you this. More than anything, I want you pregnant with my child. For you, for me...for us. It's gut-wrenching that I'll never get to see this grow." His hand falls to the couch, lifeless, his tone muted. "*Sirena*, I think it might be over. I-I don't want to give up, but I'm worried about you too. How many more of these tests can you take? How much hope do we continue to cling to for nothing?"

I cup his face, making him look at me instead of my useless stomach.

"I asked the doctors about the possibility of in vitro fertilization. Another woman's egg, my sperm, your body. There's about a fifty percent consensus on that, if it'll work or not." He shudders, eyes shutting. "I-I can't take the risk of losing you, Ariella. Don't ask me to do that. Seems most of the doctors think your body might reject the egg, and then we're stuck in another whirlwind of pain."

I haven't admitted but once I debated the same. Somehow, I knew this would be the response anyway.

Back to staring at my stomach, Erico reaches into his coat pocket and tugs out his cell. He unlocks it, clicks on the screen for a couple seconds, and then hands it to me before lifting to his feet and pacing away, letting me read it.

> Dear Mr. & Mrs. Rossi,
> Your adoption application has been completed
> and is approved. Please set up a time to
> discuss options.
>
> **New York Adoption Agency**

He's mentioned this once. The possibility of adopting his heir instead of creating one. Back then, everything was a pipe dream. So far away.

"Wh-what is this?"

Erico faces me again, hands stuffed in his pocket. "An option. Doesn't have to be now. Today. This year. But I want you to have any possible option because it's killing me I can't give you the gift I truly want."

Earlier tonight, Aurora was telling me about the underprivileged children she works with. Given it's winter, the community garden is closed, but she and Rafael, who's always had a hand in supporting the place, set something up for the winter months. She spoke about the children, not all them with families to return to, and it hit me.

How many children are in this world that need someone? Anyone.

Who are born into shit situations and don't have life's chances when they're discarded by their families.

My own father was never in the picture. Took off as soon as Mom declared she was pregnant with me, but Della and I had Mom, so it was okay.

Some kids don't even have one parent.

Then I was upset with myself for selfishly crying about producing a child myself when there's so many already out there who need me.

Then I realized wanting my own, one I created, wasn't selfish at all. It just is.

It isn't anything because you're useless, my inner demonic voice speaks for the first time all day. Guess this means the shadows are returning on one of the best days I've ever lived.

I reread the email, using it to ground myself. To consider what this truly means for Erico and me.

"How much money did it take for you to get a quick approval?" Not even counting the background check he would have had to bury. Mobster, by adoption agency's standards doesn't scream *suitable parent.*

"Does it matter?"

"No."

Erico crosses to my side again, this time sitting beside me. He takes my hands and says, "There's more."

"Oh, god."

"Not bad." He stares at the phone. "Look, if we're realistic, the tests we've been running, they're not changing anything. I can get more opinions on the IVF route. Or we adopt. Pregnancy might not be possible... but motherhood is. That I can give you." I open my mouth but he presses a finger against it, shutting me up. "I'm not done. This seems quick, I know, and you don't need to make a decision now, but," he inhales sharply, "the day after the agency got back to me, I had a soldier approach asking for time off. His seventeen-year-old teenage daughter found out she's pregnant and wasn't handling it well. She already made the decision to not abort, but will be putting up the child up for adoption." He stops, letting it all sink in.

Seventeen. Pregnant. A child herself. She'll have a newborn who'll be put right into the system.

It's an offer. He didn't state it, but I comprehend the hidden meaning. A soldier's grandchild as the next possible Rossi heir. It can stay quiet though, be within the *Famiglia*. A child available so easily to us.

"I haven't said anything to him obviously." His thumb strokes over my hand. "And she could still change her mind throughout the pregnancy. But if not, this would mean a child in less than a year. We never spoke about a timeline, so of course, if you want to wait a few years... Ariella, tell me what to do."

I can't.

There's so much.

Too much.

I imagine the soldier's teen daughter though, remembering when I was that age. Aware of life's harsh realities but not the complete extent of them. She's probably so scared, imagining all the ways her future's changed once she took that pregnancy test.

I kiss him.

"Can I think about it?"

"Of course." Erico brushes my hair over my shoulder and presses another kiss there, then to my forehead before helping me up. "Anything you want, Ariella."

I lead him to the door. "I want to return to the party for now before Della wonders why we've left for so long."

He lets me lead him out of the room, but I keep the pace slow, mind scrolling over everything we just talked about before I'm forced to wear my mask again in front of everyone. Can't let the numerous people in there see through my troubled thoughts and know something's upsetting me. Not today. Not on a day so enjoyable for everyone.

Seventeen. It wasn't that long since *I* was seventeen.

What would I do in the girl's position if that happened to me? If I wasn't as careful with protecting myself, or as open with my mother who put me right on birth control after getting with my first serious boyfriend.

If I peed on a pregnancy stick one day and saw the plus sign or the LCD screen flashing with *positive*?

Maybe I wouldn't have wanted to give the baby up, but I think I might have. Mom, Della, and me were struggling financially as it was. Bringing a baby into the household when another family could have given it a better life would have been the unselfish, motherly thing to do for my child. To release them to grant them a life better than what I'd be able to give.

To a loving couple who'd cherish the baby better than I could. A couple like Erico and me.

Erico opens the door to the sitting room again, but I stop him with a hand to his arm. "Wait. After the holidays, I want to meet her. Your soldier's daughter. I-I think we can help her."

"I think so too, *sirena*. I think so too." He drops a kiss to the top of my head, breathing my hair in deeply. "I'm so fucking sorry, Ariella."

I shake my head, taking his hand again. "No more apologies. No more regret. Just a future."

HAWKE
&
WILLOW

"H**i**."

What the fuck am I doing? Why did I do this to myself? Why did I let Willow talk me into—

My parents turn around, both with identical expressions of shock. If I whipped out a gun this instance, it'd be less of a surprise. To be honest, I'm right there with them, feeling the same.

Not only the surprise at myself that I'm here, but with a feeling of being sick. Of the ground rocking beneath my feet, of the walls caving in, as every single instance I've spent nearly two decades running from comes crashing around me.

That's putting aside the fact that every eye in this room is on us. Subtly, as they pretend not to be watching, but it's unavoidable. Willow out of support. Nico, Rafael, and Aurora out of their own conflicted and confused familial emotions. Everyone else out of a careful curiosity.

"H-hi, Hawke." My mother rests the glass she had in her hand to the table and rubs her palms along her rich dress. She licks her lips twice before glancing at my father, who, despite all the shit he's done and seen in his lifetime as the Corsetti organization's Boss, wears a completely broken expression.

"Hi," I repeat, shuffling my feet. I've been less nervous in court when facing known murderers with a very miniscule trail of evidence to help me convict them. "I, um...I—I'm sorry." It's the first thing I spit out, even if they're words I don't completely mean, so the second my mother's about to comment, I interrupt her with a rushed, "I mean, I'm not *sorry*, but I'm...sorry. I don't know...I'm..." I sigh, the truth finally piecing together in my head, able to be said in a comprehensible sentence. "I'm done. I can't do this anymore."

"Do what?" My father speaks for the first time. He clutches my mother's hand and in the corner of my eye, I catch Nico hovering a few feet closer.

"This," I reply with a long sigh. "There are no words to describe how much I hated you when I was a scared child, pleading for his father to save him. Being letdown by the very man who'd always spent so much energy placing his job above all else."

"Hawke—"

I hold up my hand to end my father's explanation. That's not why I've come over here. Not why I've spent the entire evening replaying the conversation I've been having with Willow all week. The build-up of all these visits when the realization hit, and it hit fucking hard. Harder than a courtroom gavel but with as much impact on my life.

If I'm going to continue visiting my brothers here in Montreal, my parents will be around and nothing I nor Nico can do will effectively ever one hundred percent alter that truth. But at some point, I need to continue healing.

"There will never *ever* be a time in my life I'll spin what happened to me as a positive instance. It's not, and I'll never forget what happened. But positive things came from it, like a domino effect." I manage to look away, toward Willow, meeting her eyes when I explain, "I would have been in Nico's role, if you saved me right away, or if I was never kidnapped. If I never ran away. Honestly," I face my parents again, "I wouldn't have been happy. It'd be a life without Willow. A life in which I'm not a lawyer and wouldn't have met the friends I have. In some fucked-up way, I can't completely hate the history I've survived because it gave me the present I'm thriving in. The future I'll be allowed to create."

My mother's brows are low, her eyes lined with liquid and hope. My father's lips are pressed together, his grip on my mother's hand seeming so tight, it'd break her hand soon if I don't hurry and explain everything.

"The future I'll create is why I'm here today. Why I let Willow talk me into attending Nico's wedding. Why I stayed here for days longer, until Aurora awoke from her coma. It was the life I discovered by Willow's side that I realized, while she's everything I want, she's not all I *can* have. I miss my family. Nico, Rafael, and Aurora. I vowed to Aurora after she woke up that I wouldn't go anywhere. And I won't. I refuse to let history split the four of us up again.

"But they're not all who can be included in my future. My siblings are a huge part, sure...but not the only." I pause, taking in a staggering breath before my encore. "My future is unfolding around me. Willow, my friends, my firm, my siblings...and you." I pause again, *really* wishing I downed a few shots of alcohol before this. I look to my mother and refer to her as, "Mom," and then look to my father and address, "Dad. I'm done. I won't forget what happened, won't forgive your actions or ever excuse them, but I want you in my life again. I want you there when I finally marry my girl. I want my parents to look upon the life I've created and feel proud that though I'm not a mafia boss, I'm happy. I want my parents to meet my friends. I want my *entire family*—you two, my siblings, my friends—in my life. To be a part of your lives. I won't say sorry for the things I've said or the way I've acted these past months, but from here on out, I promise I won't hold it over our relationship again."

For a full minute, no one moves. My parents stare, with almost glassy eyes, as though unable to comprehend my words.

And then Mom falls forward onto my father's shoulder, a loud sob embedding into my heart in a way I never thought it would or could. "Hawke, my boy...*thank you*."

Dad wraps an arm around her waist, but he's slowly shaking his head at me. "You were never not a part of this family, son, but the gift you've given us today can never be reciprocated. There are no words for the mistakes I made when you were a child, I know that. There's not even words to explain how grateful we are to be given this second chance. Nothing but thank you."

Mom lifts her head from his shoulder and steps toward me, her eyes darting the area, over the others murmuring quietly to themselves and to Willow. It's with her staring at my girl, she says, "When you were born, it was one of the greatest days of my life. I always dreamed of you running the family after your father, but now that you're grown, that you're *you*, I can't imagine you being anyone else. *With* anyone else. She's a lovely girl," she smiles fondly, "and I'd love to get to properly meet her too."

Considering every time my parents were in the same room as Willow, I built a wall around her. After what happened to me, after knowing what this family's like, and most importantly, after her own traumatic experiences, I'd slaughter this entire city before she's taken from me again. But now, I can build a gate into that wall and prop it open to let them through to her.

"I think she'd like that," I finally whisper.

Mom looks to me again, taking another step. Her eyes go to my arms, and then my face. "C-can I hug you?"

I stare at the foot and a half of space between us, which shrinks with every breath, even if neither of us is move. A hug might be too much right now, considering every nerve inside me is confused between the instinct to run and the instinct to embrace my parents.

So I don't hug her, but I do allow her to embrace my arms. Above her head, I find Willow on a couch across the room and meet her smile.

I love you, I mouth to her.

She owns every breath I take, every beat of my heart, every thought passing in my head.

She owns *me*.

She saved me.

The moment Caterina rests her hand on Hawke's arm, I know it'll be all right, and I want to cry immediately at the love around me. The family, boisterous and loud, but with so much care for one another.

I think back to the moment I was sitting in Hawke's bed and he told me his true past identity. Not a Blackwood, but a Corsetti, and the description he'd given this family. Then, how he reacted to Nico arriving on his doorstep after saving me for the second time. The chilling attitude as he fought to keep his past and present separated, even while they were colliding. Colliding then, and continued so, right up to Nico and Della's wedding. At every collision, something broke. Shattered. The pieces fell to the ground and waited to be put back together. Might not have happened right away, but now, it has, and that's what I'm watching now.

This isn't the family Hawke first described, and while I'm certain I'm only seeing one element of it—and not the gritty, criminal activities they participate in—this is the side that matters. Who cares that Hawke's brothers go out and deal drugs and weapons? At the end of the day, in some people's views, that makes them no different than Hawke putting away criminals during court. They're on opposite sides, enemies of one another; yet, at the end of the day, they come together.

A job is simply that. A job. As long as no one here has a basement full of captive women, I personally can look away from the questionable morals, even if Hawke doesn't think I'm strong enough to handle these people.

There's no handling, though. There's never been a need to.

As though called on him, Hawke glances over from where he's speaking with his parents, and his eyes almost twinkle in the background of the Christmas lights. Like my beautiful angel that he's always been.

Two figures join me on the couch, one on either side, and suddenly, I find myself framed by two Corsettis: Nico and Rafael. Hawke notices too but he doesn't react besides a slight widening of his eyes. That alone makes me breathe. Two months ago, he would have been losing his shit over this.

"Don't worry," Rafael reassures me as he kicks a leg over the other. "Big bro will start a fight in your honour if we harm you. You have nothing to fear."

"I know that," I smirk at Hawke's youngest brother, "but I doubt Hawke would defeat both of you."

He shrugs, angling himself so he's facing me. "Guess we'll never find out."

I look from him to the mob boss to my right, who's only scanning the room. "What brings you two over here? Other than tormenting him." I nod toward Hawke, and Nico's sharp gaze flicks right over to his older brother.

"Wanted to thank you, Willow. I don't think we've ever gotten the chance to speak alone so while Hawke's occupied, we decided now's the best time." He pause, his hands rubbing over his slacks. "Thank you for bringing our brother back to us."

Oh. "Oh, no, he did that all on his own."

"No," Nico says with finality. "He didn't. We'd be dumb to think otherwise. He wouldn't have come to the wedding if it wasn't for you. And I'm sure you urged him to come here today."

Yes, but with less effort than I believed it'd take. Almost like Hawke was battling with the deep-seated belief he had to say no, while his desires were to instead join the holiday celebration, which made my task less difficult.

It helped that none of our friends are around this year either. Ryker and Elena are spending Christmas with Ryker's family; Tristan and Natalie are finally taking a well-deserved vacation to the Bahamas; Brent and Teagan are staying with Brent's parents, leaving us free to do what we wanted. While offered to join both Ryker and Brent's families, it felt more appropriate for Hawke to rejoin his own.

"He's changed my life for the better too," I admit softly. "He saved me. Felt right to do the same for him."

Rafael leans forward until he's in my view again. "That's our point, Willow. Losing Hawke as a child broke me, so you didn't only save him. You saved all of us, and we owe you a debt no one can ever repay. If you need *anything*, god, just ask and we'll be there."

Nico, still staring at his parents, comments, "You made the impossible happen. It's one thing for him to be here with us, but that," he nods toward the trio, "that's not instant. That's a work-in-progress, only occurring because there's been multiple interactions between them. The past is slowly healing."

"That's the only way it can." My own past healed me. More so, I've healed from it, even if the scars will never fade, will be a reminder of the nightmares. "His scars will remain forever."

"Scars are survivors' marks." Nico turns a blistering stare on me, knowing, as he flicks his gaze toward my lap. "It's what's done with them after that that matters most."

Before I can respond, two arms wrap Nico's neck and Della leans over him, glancing from his face to mine. "He bothering you, Willow?" She taps his chest. "Scoot. You've had your time. My turn to talk with her."

Rafael slaps the couch and lifts to his feet as Nico shrugs his wife off and stands too. Rafael shoots me a two-fingered salute and before heading toward Isabelle, says, "Remember, Willow. Anything. Ask for the world, and I'll make it happen, since you've given me a piece of mine back."

Nico watches his brother go, and then nods at me, saying with finality, "Thank you again, Willow."

Della drops into his empty space. "Whew, that looked intense! Figured I'd save you from whatever it was."

I laugh, and we launch into a small conversation about anything. She asks about my job at Hawke's firm, and tells me about life here. Eventually, Isabelle and Aurora join in, Aurora taking the floor by my feet, so casual despite her shimmery light pink dress.

It's another twenty before Hawke interrupts, stepping dramatically over his sister, and reaching for my hands, yanking me up before I have a chance to stop him. "Excuse me all, but I need this one."

Aurora's loud laugh follows us out as Hawke propels me from the room, past a grinning Rafael, making my cheeks heat for some unknown reason. Hawke isn't dragging me off for sex, but his brother's insinuation still hits.

"Where are we going?"

Hawke, his hand firm in mine, is unyielding as he drags me through the ornate hallways, up a grand staircase that reminds me something of a castle. To think this place was once where he lived...

He pulls me through a hallway and stops at the end, in front of a door, his hand over the handle. Then he looks nervous. He licks his lips once, twice; his breath hikes, and he pulls on the knob, twisting it open.

"What are we...?" My question trails off as he steps aside as I follow him into the large bedroom. A queen-sized bed in the centre covered in a deep blue comforter. Posters of sports cars on the walls, and a large TV seated on a dresser across from it. It's not a new TV by any means, based on the thick width of it.

Wait...

"This was your bedroom," I breathe, suddenly not wanting to take a step farther into his once-private space.

Instead, he does, linking his fingers with mine, he pulls me deeper in, stopping by the bed, where he's intently studying the room around us, finally answering, "Yes. Untouched, according to my parents. Left alone all these years, on some hope I'd return. It felt right, after that, to come here."

That being his conversation. I want to ask how it went but I also want him to tell me on his own terms, when he's ready. There was no arguing and running off, so I assume well enough. I release his hand and rub my hands up either of his arms, over the soft material of his suit, embracing him.

"I needed that—" His voice cracks, and the next thing I know, I'm in his arms, his head in my neck, his arms around my waist, holding me so tight, he robs my breath. "Willow, I never fucking would have thought I'd *ever* have that conversation. Even *want* to have that conversation, but you changed my fucking life."

"You changed mine too," I reply in a soothing tone, fingers stroking through his black hair.

"I didn't know," he mumbles into my neck. "I never fucking knew they still had some claim on a part of me. But they did. It's like you said. Forgetting and forgiving are two different things."

My arms tighten, holding as much as my small form allows for until he finally lifts his head and I spot the redness around his eyes. He smiles sadly and presses a longing kiss to my forehead, breathing in sharply before releasing me.

"I wanted to bring you here, so you can see the rest of me, Willow. Where I came from. What I began as."

I rest my hand over his heart, where a tattoo should be had he chosen a different lifestyle.

"I know who you are, Hawke. You're the man I love. Your past, your present, they all make up *you*. Everything else doesn't matter."

He stares at me for a beat, his eyes blanker than I've ever seen. Then he blinks, and I'm back in his arms again, his head buried in my neck. "I fucking love you, *bella ragazza*. I owe you the fucking world for what you've done for me."

"Lucky for you, I don't need the world. Only you."

NICO
&
DELLA

NICO

Everyone gathers in the foyer to say goodnight, even though most are sleeping here tonight. Originally, the Rossi couples were going to fly home, but both Yasmine and Ariella clung to seeing their sisters for longer than a day.

So Ariella waves goodnight to everyone, hugs her sister, and leads Erico upstairs toward her old bedroom. A guest room beside them had been put aside for Caladin and Yasmine, who follow close behind.

Flynn's standing by the door, staring at his feet as Rozelyn continues her conversation with Aurora, so I sidle closer, propping myself against the wall.

"Hey, glad you came." He despises crowds, and though there's been a friendly connection half our lives, Flynn's found himself more involved lately, and when it comes to family events, he's here for both my parents and Rozelyn.

"Me too." And he sounds almost genuine as his gaze lifts from the ground. "I came for her."

"But you stayed for you."

"Yeah." He licks his lip, nodding. "Yeah, I think I did."

Rozelyn breaks away from her conversation and approaches slowly, her eyes on me. After months of her by Flynn's side, things are less strained between us, particularly the details regarding the troubled past. What happened will never be held against her again, but I think the distance between us now comes down to basic personality differences. We're amicable, though, and sometimes, downright tease one another. Like dysfunctional siblings.

"Ready for bed?" she asks Flynn.

Before he can respond, I gesture toward the staircase that the Rossi couples went up, and Aurora and Rosen are standing by. "You can take a spare room, if you'd like. No reason to go back to the soldiers' quarters."

Flynn shakes his head. "Nah, with everyone gone for the holidays, Rozelyn wanted a trip back there." He reaches for her hand and the two walk away with a final murmured goodbye. They stop by my parents, but motion by the staircase snags my attention.

Rosen's waving goodnight, but Aurora breaks from his side and bounds over to me, an infectious grin lighting up her face. She's been like a child today, but I love it. It gives insight to how badly my parents screwed up her past, but she's here now, so it's all that matters.

Aurora pulls me down in a tight hug. "I loved today. Every second of it. We should do this for New Year's. And St Paddy's. Canada Day, of course. And perhaps even Thanksgiving. Oh! And a kickass Halloween party." Her eyes bounce over the mansion. "Damn, this place would look *awesome* done up with spooky décor."

While, at first, I'm about to deny her excited suggestions, I shut myself up because they're not a bad idea. Maybe not so many gatherings because I doubt the Rossis will want to leave the U.S. that often, but some of them, perhaps. A Halloween party sounds intriguing, and maybe Canada Day to break up the year.

I untangle her arms, studying my baby sister's face. "I think we can manage more celebrations, yeah."

In truth, it's not only for her. It's for Della and Ariella, who didn't have the easiest childhood with a hardworking mother struggling to meet their basic needs. Or Flynn, who was raised by an abusive father.

And to a point, for Erico and Caladin, for Rafael and myself, all raised by mafia leaders. Couples so intent on crime, they forgot they had children at home.

Christmases with my parents were strained and unlike today. There was never other holiday celebrations. This place was never done up for Halloween or inviting friends over for Canada Day barbeques.

I find Della across the way who meets my gaze instantly, our instincts for one another always able to find the other. There will be a child—maybe multiple—in this household one day. And that's only from us. Who knows how many my siblings will bring along? For the children entering my home, they will know happiness and joy on holidays through a large family and celebrations and presents.

"Yeah," I repeat, finally looking back to Aurora. "For now, let's finish this one." I drop a kiss to her forehead and release her to Rosen.

Hawke and Willow go from my parents to my side, Hawke's arm stretching for a shake, which I return.

"I was so convinced you'd be begging me to take you to the plane."

He smiles fondly at Willow before hugging her to his side. "Me too, but I want a damn good breakfast tomorrow and I know this place serves the best." He glances over his shoulder at our parents, and then murmurs, "It's one of many things I've missed."

I rest my hand on his shoulder and hunch, so what I say remains between the three of us. "You've been missed too. This never felt like home. Not for a long time, but today I've realized everything that was missing. What you did..."

He waves his hand. "I'm sure a therapist would enjoy picking me apart, but it was time, Nico. Time to start letting go. I won't forgive their actions, won't ever forget. But like Aurora, there is a point where I need to move on. I miss them—miss all of you, and we all make mistakes. Something I never believed I'd ever be saying in reference to them." He pauses, gaze shifting to the side in thought. "As a lawyer, I've seen a lot of good people take the fall for actions and crimes they truly did commit, but sometimes, they're merely stupid errors. Mistakes, as they're being convicted, they willingly take on the punishment, knowing full well what they've done. Some have told me, they prefer prison to the outside world for a few months, few years. Gives them a chance to start over, think about where in life they fucked up, and move on by changing the future." He pauses again. "For my future to change for the better, I had to release some of my hate. I wouldn't take it back now."

Very few instances in life have rendered me speechless. Most times included Della. But this...this makes the list too. I yank him in a large, brotherly hug, causing Willow to chuckle at Hawke's gruff squeak. He's stiff in my arms for a few beats, and then returns my hold.

"We can always use a good lawyer in the family, you know. Move your friends out here."

He pulls back, catching my sly grin. He won't because he's too close to his friends, but a part of me wishes. Hell, I'll build them all one large mansion of their own that the eight of them can live in.

Before stepping back, he shoves into my shoulder playfully. "Careful now. Don't push your luck. I still want nothing to do with criminal activity."

"You'll still be on the good guys' side."

"Pfft." He rolls his eyes. "For now, my answer's no."

For now. Powerful words. From the same guy who said he'd never return, never speak with any of us, never make up with our parents. A lot of *nevers* that got smashed down. Which means *for now* doesn't have a fucking shot.

My parents wave goodnight once Willow and Hawke head upstairs and turn down toward the greenhouse Father once had built for Mother. It's also been the place Della and I have claimed, but since they visit it so infrequently now, I tug Della the opposite way, toward the ballroom.

She wraps an arm around my waist, hugging me from the side. "I never thought I'd be this happy, Nico. Truly happy."

Saying goodnight to everyone was oddly more emotional than usual, considering they're all people familiar to me. Perhaps because once morning comes, I'll have to do it again but for good. Ariella and Yasmine will return to New York with their husbands. Everyone else will go back to work, myself included, and this is all over until the next time we get together.

Nico walks me to the ballroom, our fingers interlaced together. With my hand, he spins me, reminding me so much of the time he brought me here to propose. And like that time, my spin ends with me in his arms, swaying to the imaginary sounds in our heads, the beat of our hearts.

"You've smiled so much today," he comments.

"To the point my face hurts," I joke, but the smirk accompanying it pulls against the muscle strain. "Seriously, the only thing that'd make it better is having my mother here. And Roz's mom. The way they talk about her, she wasn't anything like their father. Or, maybe not. If they were here, I wouldn't be. None of us would be. Mom wouldn't have met Stefano if his wife survived. You and I wouldn't have met."

His arm tightens around my waist and he delicately says, "I'm a selfish man, *petite souris*, and I'm sorry but I wouldn't give you up for anything in the world. Your mother included."

His promise warms my heart because it's all I can truly ask for.

Nico swings me around in two more arcs before admitting, "My parents asked me three times today about your pregnancy."

He means my lack of. For all the joy, I'm suddenly cold in a way Montreal's freezing outdoor temperatures have nothing to do with.

"What'd you tell them?"

"The truth. That you're not yet."

"They'll ask again."

He shrugs. "So they will. You're all that matters." His hand tightens around mine, his steps slowing to a barely-there sway. "If you've changed your mind and want children earlier, I'm not opposed, but I'm personally still sticking to our previous decision."

"Same," I admit in a low voice, taking my hand from his to cup his face instead. "I love you, Nico, but we haven't even *known* each other for a complete year. I really want it to only be you and me for another two or three years before we bring kids into the mix."

His hands come up to rest over my own. "Della, we're going to see the world together first. Every corner of it. And then, when we've returned, we'll have a shortlist of places to explore with our children in the future." He pauses, his gaze drifting to the door. "Aurora really enjoyed today. It was her first Christmas home and she recommended more events like this to bring us all together. It got me thinking about us all, who can benefit from that. Then I also considered our children. I want them to run around this place and know only joy. To see their large, fucked-up family come together for these events. To have a place with fond memories. This mansion's held so much hate over the past few decades between Hawke leaving, Aurora being sent off, and Raf and I simply surviving with what's left. That's not what our children will have. Ours, or any nieces and nephews that come our way."

His words take my gaze away from his face. To the ballroom around us, imagining it decked out for parties and Halloween and even birthdays. To little children running around. To them having the life Mom always dreamed of having for us but it all being out of reach.

"I want that too," I reply softly. "Not yet...but soon. You realize, that's another two or three Christmases of your parents asking, right?"

He shrugs. "Then that's two or three times of me saying 'not yet.' They'll live."

They'll live but the organization will hate me. From the second we were wed, the expectations have been there. Nico might have siblings, but as Boss, he's who they're looking to for the heir.

Just like Ariella.

Poor Ariella. Even having this conversation feels like a betrayal.

My hands drop to my stomach. "I think I should get tested, though. After what happened to Ariella, I'm scared that when we do decide it's time for me to get off birth control and try to conceive, we'll have the same outcome, and I can't..." Even finish, apparently. "I can't be ready after years of putting it aside, to decide now's the time to make an heir, all to discover my body won't allow it."

He frowns. I see it in his gaze, he wants to deny me, but he can't because I'm right. I could very well have the same struggles as my sister and we'd be in her and Erico's precise position.

He covers my hand with his large one, granting me a hint of what it'll feel like in years to have him hold our child with me. "I don't want you to go through that, but I hear you. Logically, it's smart because then we can prepare for that outcome."

"You mean for when the organization despises me."

It's a joke, but his deadly eyes narrow to slits, his hand becoming heavier over mine. "The entire organization can crash and burn before I lose you, *petite souris.* Trust me, you're not going anywhere. We'd figure it out, like your sister and Erico are." A grin shatters the serious topic and he tugs me into his chest again. "Besides, I spent *way* too much effort chasing your ass across the country to let you go. You realize how many resources I've spent on you?"

I laugh, thankful for the break in topic, and pull him down into a heated kiss. It's a peck, soon driven by hunger, desire, and a passion only he entices in me. His tongue strokes against mine at the precise second something chimes in the background. His kiss in line with the bell's dings.

Ding dong... ding dong...

He pulls away, grinning. "Well, look at that. Midnight. What a perfect time to give my wonderful queen her present."

I pace back two steps, already knowing without asking. My heartbeat quickens, my palms getting sweatier, my lungs preparing for the run. "Oh yeah? What's that?"

He bears down on me, a single step before shedding his outer coat and rolling up his sleeves, revealing muscled arms.

"Run, *petite souris,* run. And don't make it easy."

"Never."

LORENZO

&

CATERINA

LORENZO

L ate at night, after everyone's gone to bed, I lead Caterina to the greenhouse I once had erected for her.

Hawke and Willow, Rafael and Isabelle, Aurora and Rosen, Ariella and Erico, and Flynn and Rozelyn each are sleeping in their old rooms, while Yasmine and Caladin took a guest room. The entire family is beneath one roof, and it feels fucking amazing. As a father, as the ex-Boss, as a man, there's a pride in being able to comfortably settle into one's home, knowing only love, devotion, and loyalty.

The greenhouse is chilly, considering it's the end of December, but the heaters in here allow the space to be as temperature-controlled as possible without ruining the plants. Still, I remove my outer coat and drop it over my queen's shoulders.

The woman who's been by my side through everything. Every rampage, every battle, every contract. Four beautiful children and a lifetime of ups and downs all because my uncles admitted the truth of our childhood engagement and I was certain to steal back that future.

As Boss, I've had numerous regrets. Ones relating to the organization, and many about my children, but Kitty Cat has never been one.

Not since the moment I snuck into her bedroom all those years ago, on the day of her wedding to a Rossi.

I remember pausing at the entranceway, and staring at the woman I'd seen only in newspaper photos thus far. She was beautiful in that wedding dress, even if it looked all wrong on her. There was an innocence to her that I craved stealing for myself.

Turns out, she became my heart, and that's what was reflecting back in that mirror she stood in front of that day.

Like many times before, I lead her to the fountain, sitting first and pulling her onto my lap. She winds her arms through the coat, wearing it properly, and then wraps them around me. I hold onto her legs, rubbing my palms up and down her thighs to keep them warm.

"There's a satisfaction in one's life after a day like today," I tell her. "When seeing my family around the table, together. Gaining our first son back, even when prior mistakes mean we don't deserve Hawke's forgiveness at all."

"I'm so happy he gave it," Caterina cuts in, her hand resting over my steady beating heart. "I couldn't live another year without him back in our lives."

"In time," I remind her. Today was a start, but nowhere close to the finish line. "It'll only get better from here."

"Willow," she murmurs softly. "Such a lovely girl. A dark past, but a fighting spirit. Do you see how he is with her? If she looks away, he does too. Moves when she does. They're magnets for one another."

I did notice, and I saw myself in my eldest son. I might have not had a hand in raising him for the second half of his life, but the way he loves his woman is the way I love his mother.

"He's so different than the child we betrayed," Caterina comments, "but in some ways, it worked out for the best. He's the better version of himself, Enzo. I truly don't think he'd be who he is had we protected him. He'd be running the family now, but he wouldn't be as free or as happy."

No, I silently agree. He wouldn't. My son never hid his hatred of the mob life even as a child, but the man I watched sitting at the table today, continuously touching Willow, laughing with his brothers had a sense of lightness and freedom emitting from him. A willingness to be around, aware that he gets to return to a different home, with different friends who deserve him, and his own law firm. Set out to right the wrongs in the world. Everything opposite of what this organization stands for; yet, he succeeds in making it work.

"I'll forever thank you, Kitty Cat, for forcing me to bring home Flynn after we found him between the buildings. A wounded soul, that in some ways, filled the gap left by Hawke."

She nods, smiling sadly. "We did right by him, but he's done right by us more. I'm pleased he and Rozelyn found their way back to one another. He deserves her. And she's not so bad, putting aside her father's actions." Despite the travesty of the situation we dealt with, Caterina chuckles. "If our children are no longer holding our mistakes against us, we'd be hypocrites to do the same to someone else's."

"Rafael's blooming as underboss, and soon, he'll have Isabelle to call his wife. Aurora, another child we did wrong by who forgave us; she's so happy with Rosen. Honestly, after seeing them together, and then Erico today," the admittance is rough in my throat, "they would have killed each other."

"It really did work out for the best. If there's one child to most be proud of, it'd be Nico." She tips her head to me. "You raised him perfectly, Enzo."

"*We* did."

"He's a fantastic leader for all of them. And Della, she's ideal for him."

"The Corsettis will live on. With Della by his side, Nico will lead the family forward, with a connection to the *Famiglia,* to boot. Ariella... damn she's a strong one." I'd like to say fucking over Rossi's uncle way back when was a mistake, but it'll never be for everything we just listed out. If I never sliced a man's neck, I wouldn't have found Caterina, and all of that wouldn't have come to pass.

"We made a good life," she agrees, smiling up at me. "A life better than I ever could have imagined. I'm so happy I fell in love with the villain."

CATERINA

There comes a point in every woman's life when they determine if they've fucked up their relationship or did right by it.

I never had that moment. Lorenzo has been it for me the moment he forced me into marriage. A struggle, a battle, I later realized was pointless in even having.

Almost forty years later, I wouldn't change anything for the world. Not the battle with my family, not our marriage, not the years after. The children we had.

I suppose, I'd alter one thing if I could: Hawke's treatment. But I'd want to leave a note from my future self to past self. Save him, but release him too. Because to release him from the mob, from his oaths, *was* saving him. Maybe then, we wouldn't have lost years with our son, but he still needed to grow into the man he's become. His business, his friends, Willow. They're a part of him and chaining him down to this organization would have destroyed him.

I'm holding Enzo as tight as I can as I study the greenhouse garden that's been privy to so many conversations between him and me. Hell, Hawke might have been even conceived here. Aurora too, I think. By the time three boys were around, finding quiet time was more difficult.

My sister once told me to find the best in Enzo, and every day, her wise advice from such a young age sticks with me. Advice even given to others, like Ariella on the morning of her wedding to Erico Rossi. I doubt my sister's aware of the impact her words have, even to this day.

I snuggle into his neck again, staring at the moon above. "Do you remember when you first built this greenhouse?"

"Mhm. Every second."

"Thank you."

He pulls back until he can see my face, brows dipping. "After all these years still?"

"Always. Always because I love you so fucking much. You and this family. Our interconnected family that somehow found itself growing within months, but damn if I'm happy they're resolving all the errors you and I once made."

He nods in agreement but doesn't reply, looking thoughtful.

"I dreamed of the happily-ever-after once, Enzo. It didn't come easy, or right away, but it came, and that's what matters."

"So many fractured endings," he muses. "Ours, Della and Ariella, the De Falco sisters, Flynn...So many broken paths, crushed dreams, endless pain that had to be put back together. Everything occurring this year has been more exhausting and more exhilarating than my entire time as boss."

"Fractured," I repeat the single word, chewing it around my mouth. "It's the best term for this year, Enzo. Fractured individuals, coming together for their happily-ever-afters. Don't you see?"

Wrapping both hands around mine, he shakes his head.

"That's what this year's been. A bunch of fractured ever afters."

And then I lean forward and kiss Lorenzo Corsetti under the white moon, beneath the stars, surrounded by the interior garden and walled with frosty snow.

My Enzo.

My kidnapper.

My husband.

My past.
My future.
My heart.
My soul.
My *everything*.

Yes, number two.

If you've been with me since the Captive Writings series, you'll recognize Hawke and Willow. If you've read book 1 & 2 of this series, you may recall them, but didn't receive *as much* of a background, since their story is Burning Notes.

But, for those familiar with him and his background, I wanted to answer a question you may have had when reading: **Why did Hawke reconnect with his parents?**

When writing Burning Notes, I linked Hawke to the mafia through his traumatic background. When writing The Hunt in Elusion, I recalled the fact that Nico has another brother—an older brother: Hawke—and mentioned him to Della. Then it only made sense for Della to encourage the wedding invite, which is where the bonus scene at the end of that book as well as his presence in The Craving in Slumber had come from.

Based on his story, The Hunt in Elusion, and The Craving in Slumber even *I* never thought he'd forgive their actions. Hawke clung to his hatred of his parents (and the mafia as a whole) for good reason. (Not discrediting this anger over the situation.)

But then came this novella, and after the ongoing building relationships with Hawke and his siblings throughout the Fractured Ever Afters series, it wasn't right to leave him out of Christmas, which is why he travelled in for the celebration.

Then he wrote his own part.

So why did I allow it?

People grow. People change. People evolve. People go through experiences differently. You might be thinking *I wouldn't ever do what he did*, and you know what? I don't know if I would either. As a therapist in my day job, I see a lot of growth and change in people, depending their own capacities, but more importantly: their wants and needs.

That is why.

Do I condone the mistakes his parents made? No. And this isn't meant to reflect such a thing.

But it's a sign of individual differences. A sign of family and the ongoing battle Hawke was tired of fighting. After so long, after reconnecting with his siblings first, which he said he'd never do, and maintaining communication, the steps were being laid. Really, Nico and Rafael explain it best in Willow's chapter: "The past is slowly healing."

If you're a Captive Writings reader, I hope you felt this crossover was suitable.

—M.L. Philpitt

Read on for some bonus fun facts about the Fractured Ever Afters series!

Get the entire Fractured Ever Afters series as a signed paperback set for your shelves. The 6 books & 2 novellas all in one bundled price. Scan to shop!

BONUS FACTS

1) I owned the cover for The Beauty in Scars even before starting this series. I always had a Beauty and the Beast mafia retelling planned and when Cat Imb (TRC Designs) posted that premade cover in her group for sale, it screamed everything I wanted. I intended for that cover/the Beauty and the Beast retelling to be book 1 of the series.

2) On a similar note, the original concept for The Beauty in Scars was actually a blend of it and The Hunt in Elusion. The character was always named Nico, always leader of the mafia, and one of his soldiers came to him begging for assistance in finding a suitable husband for his scarred daughter, Isabelle. When Nico saw her though, he wanted her for himself.

After introducing Nico in Burning Notes, it didn't feel right for his character so I scrapped the concept. Nico gave me different vibes - hunter vibes - and rather than falling in love with a shy woman, he gave me the sense he'd seek someone more like him. I took a few weeks off and was struck with the Cinderella retelling that The Hunt in Elusion became.

3) Fractured Ever Afters was never intended to become a series. It was supposed to be the standalone described above. Everything mentioned so far occurred even before Burning Notes (Captive Writings #4). When the new Cinderella idea came to me, I gave Nico siblings in order to still do my Beauty and the Beast retelling and use that cover. It was intended to be book 2. When writing Burning Notes, my brain exploded and linked Hawke to the mafia family, gave him numerous siblings, and thus, Fractured Ever Afters was born. Basically, when writing Captive Writings I NEVER thought, nor planned, the two series to be so closely linked. No regrets how it all turned out out!

4) I love every book in the series for a different reason but my favourites are The Beauty in Scars and The Sound in Silence. The Beauty in Scars for the plot, characters, and stomach-clenching feeling Raf gives me. They wrote their own book in about 2 weeks.

The Sound in Silence because I was proud of how I managed the characterizations and romance, given the character's parameters for her mutism. (Which was easier to write than initially assumed).

5) The most challenging to write was The Craving in Slumber and The Freedom in Captivity. The Craving in Slumber because it's the only novel I've (so far) had to do so many rewrites/edits on, to the point, the book published is vastly different than the first few drafts (even the "final" one, originally sent to my editor), also resulting in a changed release date. Worked out for the best though.

The Freedom in Captivity because when I started it, I had no story for the characters and floundered for a few chapters.

6) The series was intended to end at The Beauty in Scars, after all the Corsetti siblings got their stories. The De Falco plot line was supposed to start and end with Della in book 1. But after writing The Hunt in Elusion, I wanted to give Ariella a story and further explore her character, along with her stepsisters. Thus...6 books.

7) The Obscurity in Wishing began with a MUCH different plot line. Something more Aladdin inspired but it didn't work for Caladin's characterization/role/power so I changed it.

8) Flynn and Rozelyn were supposed to be strangers to one another. Not second-chance romance. Why I included their history is a secret I'll keep ;)

9) The Sound in Silence was planned to be a traditional arranged marriage romance where Erico wouldn't care for her until much later in the story. They wrote their own book and Erico told me to fuck right off with that idea.

10) Fractured Ever Afters has spun off into 3 different series, all 3 of which I've began: a novella series, another mafia series, and an academy series.

11) The series was almost about the New York mafia (which is essentially why that's where the Rossis are from). Many published mafia romances are New York-based, but I did some research into Montreal's mafia, really wanting to base my books in Canada, as my others are. But I was worried no one would read them since they're not in New York and spent hours going back and forth with my PA over this, before finally just saying *fuck it* and setting the series in Montreal.

I love that I did and I've had a lot of Canadian readers reach out to me as a result of it. Montreal was my hometown and where I did my BA, so any location mentioned is because I visited there directly either as a kid or an adult. And all my comments about bagels in book 1 & 6 was because the Faubourg on Sainte-Catherine street had the BEST bagel place when I was a child and I got a kick out of watching the production of them when we'd order. #iykyk

12) For a long time, my Google Maps history had a billion New York locations because I had to learn a whole new city for Erico and Caladin's stories... I had friends ask me if I went on a recent trip when they saw the app.

ALSO BY M.L. PHILPITT

Fractured Ever Afters

A 6-book (& 2 novellas) mafia romance series of interconnected standalones based on fairytales, featuring the Montreal mafia and the New York Famiglia.

The Desire in Deception (Prequel Novella)

The Hunt in Elusion

The Craving in Slumber

The Beauty in Scars

The Freedom in Captivity

The Sound in Silencea

The Obscurity in Wishing

The Bonds in Christmas (Epilogue Novella)

The Bratva's Elite

A 4-book mafia series of interconnected standalones featuring the Russian Bratva.

Merciless Queen

Deadly Knight

Defensive Rook

Violent Pawn

Captive Writings

A new adult suspenseful romance series that progressively gets darker with each book

Ruthless Letters

Obsessive Messages

Vicious Texts

Burning Notes

Twisted Holidays

A series of dark romance holiday novellas

Silent Night

Egg Hunt

Fright Night

Be Mine

Midnight Kiss

Lucky Clover

Black Magick

A 5-book paranormal romance series of interconnected standalones featuring witches, vampires, shifters, mortals, and demons.

Dark Flame

Dark Mist

Dark Storm

Standalones

A Vampire for Christmas

Audiobooks

Silent Night

ACKNOWLEDGMENTS

I can't be more happy with this series and a massive part of that is all you readers who've stuck by me through it. You're all appreciated more than words can say.

Since this novella was written, edited, and created concurrently with The Obscurity in Wishing, a lot of my thanks goes out to those who worked with me on not only this one but the rest of the series too:

- Betas: Megan, Colleen, & Lee Jacquot
- Editor: Rebecca Barney, Fairest Reviews Editing Services
- Assistant: Megan
- Cover Designer: Cat Imb, TRC Designs
- French Translator: Karina (@id_rather.be.the.moon)

ABOUT THE AUTHOR

USA Today Bestselling author M.L. Philpitt writes both dark romance and paranormal romance. When she's not writing made-up realities, she's reading them. She lives in Canada with her four pets and survives life with coffee and an obsession with fictional characters, especially the morally grey kind. By day, she masks as a therapist.